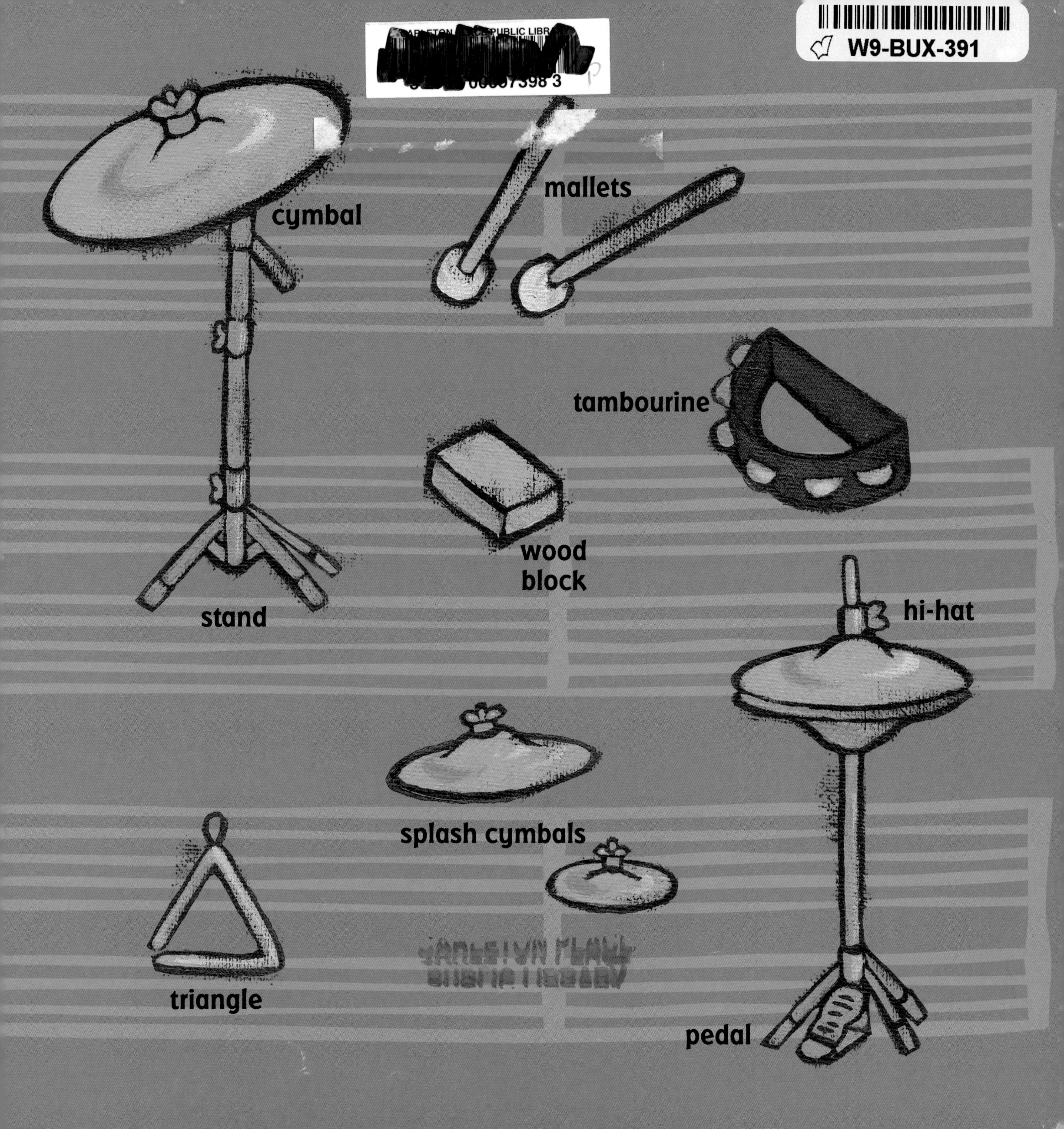
cymbal
mallets
tambourine
wood
block
stand
hi-hat
splash cymbals
triangle
pedal

To Jason and Beck for the loud inspiration,
and Gram and Gramps for making sure everyone wears ear protection!

 First edition 2011. Library of Congress Cataloging-in-Publication Data is available. Library of Congress Catalog Card Number 2010044814. ISBN 978-0-7636-4477-2. Printed in Shenzhen, Guangdong, China. This book was typeset in Badger. The illustrations were done in acrylic. Candlewick Press, 99 Dover Street, Somerville, Massachusetts 02144. Visit us at www.candlewick.com. 11 12 13 14 15 16 CCP 10 9 8 7 6 5 4 3 2 1

MIKE!

LESLIE PATRICELLI

CANDLEWICK PRESS

This is a story about a monkey named Mike,
who started drumming as a tiny little tyke.

He played with his fingers;
he played with his feet—
a funky little monkey with a

beat, beat, beat.

Bing, bong, bing,
his rhythms would sing,

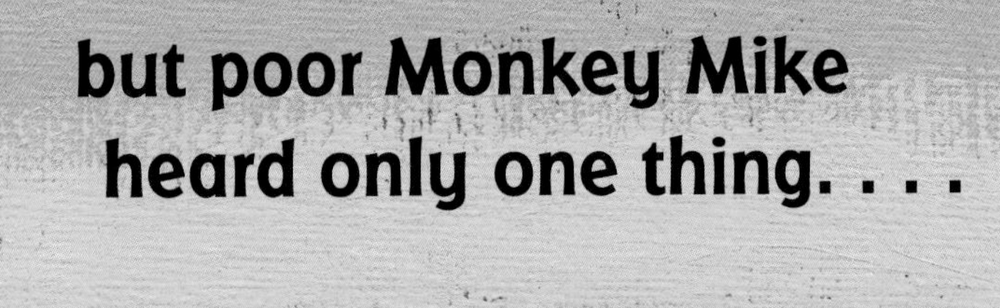

but poor Monkey Mike
heard only one thing. . . .

BANG
CLANK
CRASH
kong

He heard it from his parents;
he heard it from his sis;
he heard it from the neighbors,
and it sounded like this:

BE
QUIET,

MIKE!

"Maybe he'll grow out of it,"
said his mom and pop.
But as Mike grew older,
his rhythms didn't stop!

He played on the table
like a wild baboon.

He played on the dolls in his little sister's room.

But everywhere he played, he heard the same tune:

BE
QUIET,

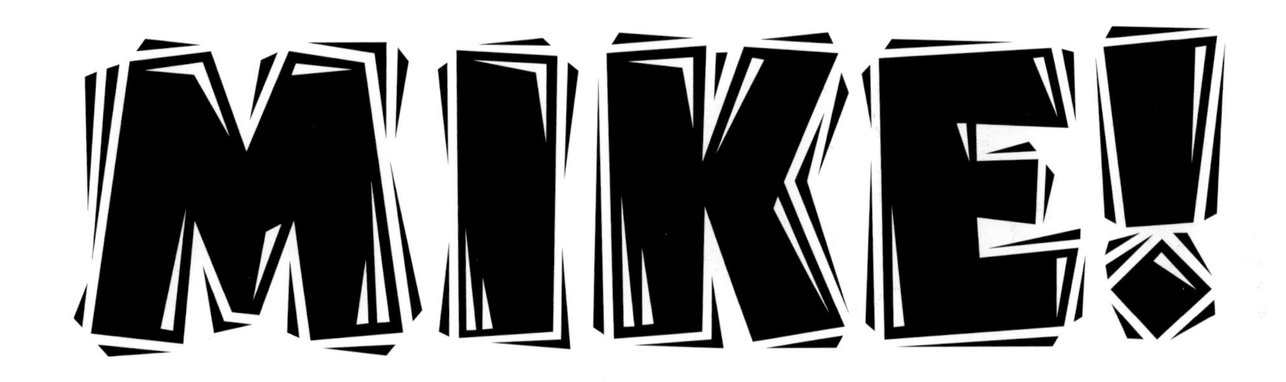
MIKE!

Mike tried to be quiet,
he tried to be still,
but the beat of his heart
was stronger than his will.

Mike was good at school—
he wasn't one for yapping,
but with pencils everywhere,
he couldn't stop tapping.

No noise was the rule
all day long.
And every single day,
he heard that same old song . . .

BE
QUIET,

MIKE!

Then one day, he was walking with his pop
when they passed by the window of a big music shop.
And that's where he saw it,
shining like a jet—

a real live, full-size

jamming drum set!

And there at the drum set,
an ape with long fur,
beating so fast—
arms and legs a blur.

He boomed on a bass drum,
rolled on a snare,
banged on a floor tom,
sticks in the air.

BOOM CHICK, BOOM CHICK, ZAT ZOOM CRASH!

HI-HAT, HI-HAT, BASS, TOM SMASH!

Mike's heart was in pieces;
he couldn't deny it.
He wanted that set,
and he just couldn't buy it.

But that *want* got him dreaming. . . .
That *need* made him think. . . .

AHA!

An idea! It arrived in a blink.

Mike took out his sketch pad
and started to draw.
His mind had a picture;
he sketched what he saw.

Then he *really* got to work—
his room was a disaster!
He ripped tape, clanged metal,
faster and faster.

When Mike was all through,
he sat down on his throne,
twirled his sticks, and . . .

made a sound all his own!

DIGGETY DIGGETY

ZAT ZOOM CRASH!

COFFEE CAN

COFFEE CAN

POT PAN SPLASH!

He rolled on his bucket,
rang on his chimes,
pulled out his bananas,
and played in double time!

Mike played so hard,
he fell off his seat—
but even on the floor,
he never missed a beat!

First chimes, then a fill,
a BOOM, then he stopped
and looked up in surprise—

it was his mom, sis, and pop!

His mom started clapping!
Then his dad, then his sis!
They hooted and they cheered,
and they blew him a kiss!

And do you know what they said?
Well, it sounded like this . . .

PLAY LOUDER

MIKE!

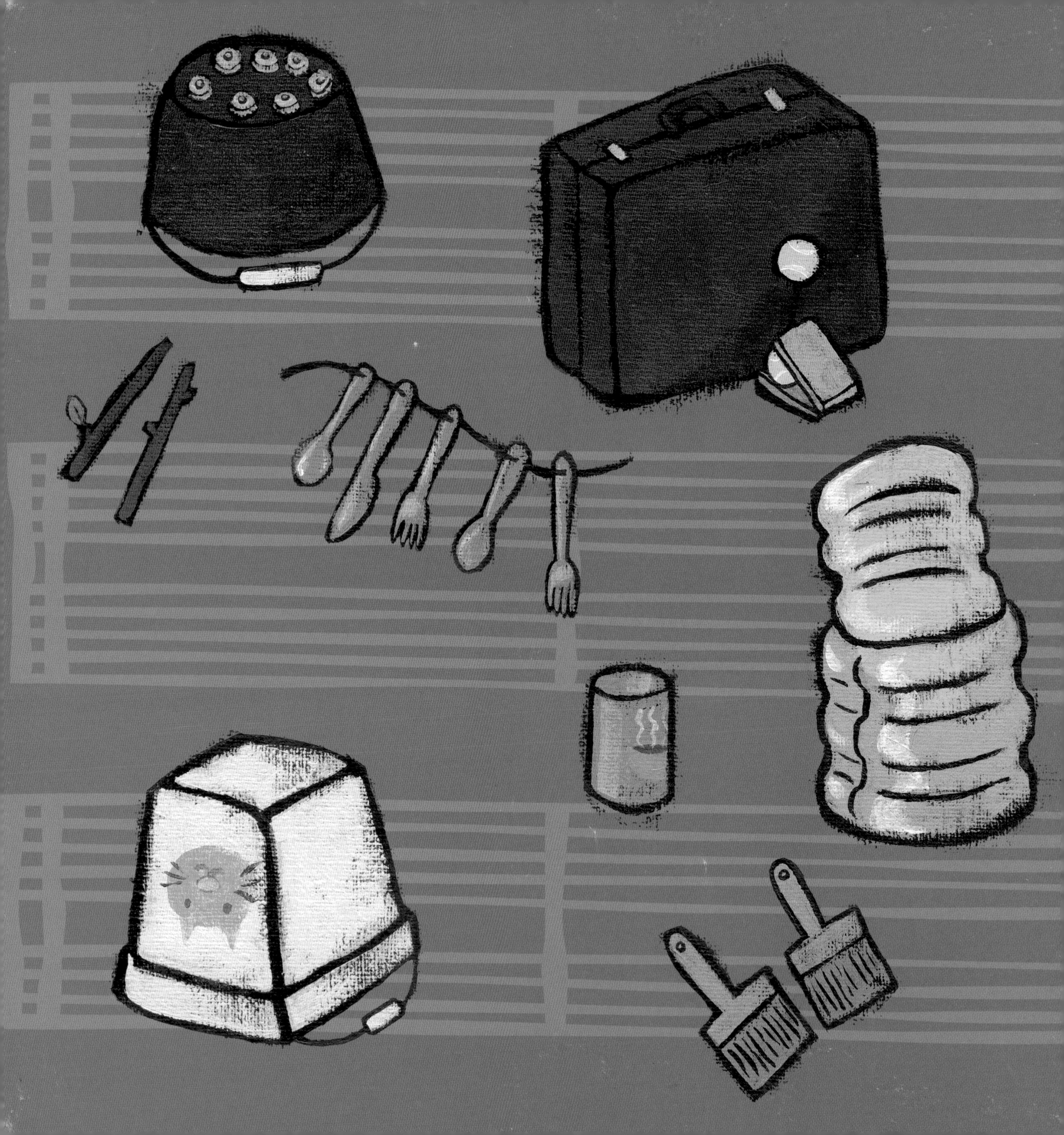